The Joy Boys

The Joy Boys

BETSY BYARS

illustrated by Frank Remkiewicz

A Yearling First Choice Chapter Book

Published by Bantam Doubleday Dell Publishing Group, Inc.
1540 Broadway
New York, New York 10036
Text copyright © 1996 by Betsy Byars
Illustrations copyright © 1996 by Frank Remkiewicz
All rights reserved.

Library of Congress Cataloging-in-Publication Data
Byars, Betsy Cromer.
    The joy boys / by Betsy Byars ; illustrated by Frank Remkiewicz.
    p.   cm.
    Summary: Two brothers share several adventures with their dog on
the family farm, riding cows, making mud bombs, and hunting for a
wild animal.
    Hardcover ISBN 0-385-32164-3 — Paperback ISBN 0-440-41094-0
    [1. Brothers—Fiction. 2. Farm life—Fiction. 3. Dogs—Fiction.]
I. Remkiewicz, Frank, ill. II. Title.
PZ7.B9836Jo 1996
[Fic]—dc20   94-33474   CIP   AC

The text of this book is set in 17-point Baskerville.

Manufactured in the United States of America

March 1996

10 9 8 7 6 5 4 3 2 1

Contents

1. The B-Bull

"No, Bono," Harry said.

"J.J. and I are going
to the cow pasture.
We're going to ride the cows."

"Yes," said J.J. "You can't come.
You might get stepped on."

"I bid for Brownie," said J.J.

"I'll take Blackie," said Harry.

The boys heard a shout behind them.

They turned.

"If you boys are going to ride the cows,"

Mr. Joy said, "don't.

I put the bull in there this morning."

J.J. turned to Harry.

"What did he say?"

"I don't know.

I think he asked

if we were going to ride the cows."

"Yes, Dad, yes," they yelled back.

They went to the cow pasture.

"We're in luck," J.J. said.

"The cows are beside the fence.

That makes it easy to get on."

The Joy boys climbed onto the fence.

J.J. got on Brownie.

Harry got on Blackie.

The cows walked away from the fence.

"Let's play like we're cowboys," J.J. said,

"and some bad guys are after us."

"Yes!" Harry said.

"I will look back," J.J. said,

"and I will see the bad guys,

and I will yell—"

He looked back.

"The b-b—" he yelled.

"That is good acting,"

Harry said.

"You do sound afraid."

J.J. said, "The b-b—"

Harry said, "I know, the bad guys."

Harry looked back then.

"Oh, the b-b—

Let's get out of here.

Come on, Blackie," he said.

"Get me to the fence."

"Come on, Brownie," J.J. said.

"Get me over there too."

The cows walked slowly.

"Please, Blackie, giddyup."

"Please, please, Brownie, giddyup."

"Please, please, please—"

"He's coming!

Run for it!" J.J. yelled.

The Joy boys slid off the cows.

They ran for the fence.

The bull ran for the boys.

The boys went under the fence.

The bull went into it.

Harry and J.J. lay on the grass.

J.J. said, "Dad was trying

to tell us about the b-b—

See, I still can't say it."

The Joy boys got up

and started down the hill.

"Come on, Bono," Harry called.

"You can come with us now.

We're through riding cows."

2. Mud Bombs

It had rained for a week.

J.J. and Harry had been waiting

to go outside for a week.

Finally the rain stopped.

"We're going out," Harry called.

Mrs. Joy called back,

"Don't get your shoes muddy."

"We won't."

They took off their shoes

and went outside.

The mud oozed between their toes.
"You know what we haven't done
in a long time?" Harry said.
"What?"
"Make mud bombs."
"Right. Let's do it!"

They made a large pile of mud bombs.

"What's our target?" J.J. asked.

"Let's play like some outlaws
have come to our ranch," said Harry,
"and we have to scare them off."

"Right," said J.J.

He pointed.

"Those trees can be the outlaws."

"That's no fun," said Harry.

"Trees don't move.

I like a moving target."

"I do too,

but nothing's moving," J.J. said.

Then he grinned.

"I'm moving!" he shouted.

"Nyah! Nyah!

You can't hit me."

Splat!

"Now it's my turn

to be the outlaw," said Harry.

"You can't hit me!"

Pow!

Splat!

"Bull's-eye!"

They threw until their bombs were gone.

J.J. said, "That was fun!"

"Right! Let's make some more,

and this time—"

"Boys!" Mrs. Joy called.

"Stop that fighting."

J.J. stopped.

He looked at Harry.

Harry looked at J.J.

"And get in this house. Now!"

Harry and J.J. walked slowly
to the house.

"She sounds mad," J.J. said.

"I don't know why, do you?"

"No. She told us not
to get our shoes muddy."

"And we didn't!"

3. The Fight

Mrs. Joy drew a line
down the middle of the boys' bedroom.
She said, "Harry, you stay on this side.
J.J., you stay on that side.
I am tired of you boys fighting."
"We were not fighting, Mom," J.J. said.

"I saw you out the window," Mrs. Joy said.

" You were having a mud fight."

"We were playing.

J.J. was the outlaw."

"I know fighting when I see it,"

Mrs. Joy said.

"And you cannot come out of this room

until you say you're sorry for fighting."

She went out of the room.

J.J. sat on his bed.

Harry sat on his bed.

They looked up.

They saw Bono in the doorway.

"Here, Bono," J.J. said.

"Come here, Bono. Good dog."

Harry said, "No, Bono,

don't go to J.J.

Come to me. Good dog."

"Come on, Bono,
don't go to Harry.
He's the one who started it."
"I did not.
You started it.

You're the one who said,
'Nyah! Nyah! You can't hit me.' "
"Well, you're the one who
wanted to make mud bombs."
"Well, you're the one who helped."

Harry threw his pillow at J.J.

J.J. threw it back.

Harry threw it harder.

The pillow broke open.

"Now look what you did!" Harry said.

"I'll get you for that."

He threw the pillow.

It hit a picture on the wall.

The picture crashed.

Bono fled.

The Joy boys looked at each other.

"I guess the fighting scared Bono,"
Harry said.

"Yes, *that* was fighting," J.J. said.

"Right. That was fighting."

"Mom!" Harry called.

"I'm sorry for fighting."

"Mom, I'm sorry too," J.J. called.

"All right, you boys can come out now."

J.J. and Harry went into the living room.

"Bono!" Harry called.

"Bono!" J.J. called.

Bono came out from behind the sofa.

"Did we scare you, Bono?

Well, we won't do it anymore, Bono."

"We're never going to fight again."

"Right!"

4. The Wild Animal

"No, Bono, you can't come with us,"
J.J. said.

"You have to go home."

Bono stopped.

His tail drooped.

"Yes," said Harry.

"A wild animal has been after our sheep.

We have to catch him.

You will be in the way."

Bono sat down.

He watched J.J. and Harry walk off.

At the trees, the boys turned.

"Now don't follow us.

We mean it."

J.J. and Harry went deep into the woods.

They stopped at the cliff.

"We can watch for the wild animal here,"

Harry said. "Let's put up the tent."

"And the campfire can go here," said J.J.

The boys worked hard,

but it got dark before supper was ready.

"We better eat in the tent," J.J. said.

Harry said, "Why?"

"Because of the wild animal."

Harry said, "What wild animal?"

"The wild animal that's after the sheep."

Harry said, "Let's go in the tent."

They ate their food in the tent.

Then they lay down.

After a while Harry said,

"I can't sleep, can you, J.J.?"

J.J. said, "No."

Harry said,

"I keep thinking about the wild animal."

"I do too," said J.J.

Harry sat up.

"What was that?" he said.

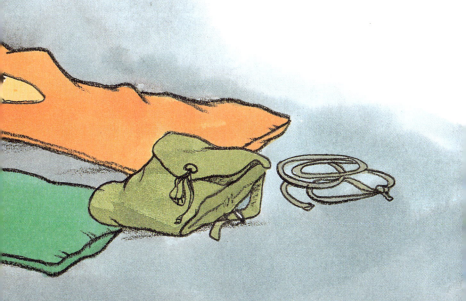

"What?"

"I heard something," Harry said.

"What?"

"It sounded like a wild animal."

They listened.

They heard footsteps.

They heard breathing.

44

The flap of the tent opened.

A long nose poked through the flap.

"Wild animal! Wild animal!"
Harry cried.

He pulled his sleeping bag over his head.

J.J. pulled his sleeping bag over his head.

They waited.

Then the long nose poked J.J.

J.J. peeked out.

"It's Bono! Bono!" he said.

"Harry, look, it's Bono.

He chased the wild animal away."

Bono lay down between the Joy boys.

"Now I can sleep, can't you?"

said Harry.

"Yes, now I can sleep," said J.J.

The Joy boys fell asleep

as Bono's tail wagged

on the floor of the tent.

Betsy Byars won the Newbery Medal for *Summer of the Swans* and the American Book Award for *The Night Swimmers*. She is also the author of the Blossom family books, the Bingo Brown books, and the popular Golly Sisters books. She lives in Clemson, South Carolina.

Frank Remkiewicz is the author and illustrator of more than twenty books for children and the illustrator of many more. He has also created many greeting cards, cartoons, and posters, as well as the box for a popular brand of animal crackers. He recently moved from Northern California to Sarasota, Florida, with his wife and daughter.